curious about

# MARTIAL ARTS

BY LISA M. BOLT SIMONS

AMICUS LEARNING

# What are you

# curious about?

CHAPTER THREE

## Competing in Martial Arts




Curious About is published by Amicus Learning, an imprint of Amicus
P.O. Box 227
Mankato, MN 56002
www.amicuspublishing.us





Editor: Grace Cain and Megan Siewert
Series Designer: Kathleen Petelinsek
Book Designer and Photo Researcher: Emily Dietz

Library of Congress Cataloging-in-Publication Data
Names: Simons, Lisa M. Bolt, 1969- author. Title: Curious about martial arts / by Lisa M. Bolt Simons. Description: Mankato, MN : Amicus Learning, 2025. | Series: Curious about sports | Includes bibliographical references and index. | Audience: Ages 5-9 | Audience: Grades 2-3 | Summary: "Conversational questions and answers share what kids can expect when they join martial arts, including what to wear, what competitions are like, and which style is best for a beginner. A Stay Curious! feature models research skills while simple infographics support visual literacy. Includes glossary and index"– Provided by publisher. Identifiers: LCCN 2023043288 (print) | LCCN 2023043289 (ebook) | ISBN 9781645497110 (library binding) | ISBN 9781681529745 (paperback) | ISBN 9781645497172 (ebook) Subjects: LCSH: Martial arts–Juvenile literature. Classification: LCC GV1101.35 .S56 2025 (print) | LCC GV1101.35 (ebook) | DDC 796.8–dc23/eng/20230929
LC record available at https://lccn.loc.gov/2023043288 LC ebook record available at https://lccn.loc.gov/2023043289

Photo Credits: Adobe Stock/ain, 22, 23; Alamy/Mark Edward Eite, 8, Split Seconds, 17; Getty/Cavan Images, 2,14, Frazer Harrison, 21, Michael Ochs/ Stringer, 21; iStock/AnnaStills, 10, 11, apfDesign, 6, artpipi, 2, 8, DanielBendjy, 9, diane555, 5, FatCamera, 5, Gerville, Cover, 1, PeopleImages, 20, slobo, 3, 16, Stefan Tomic, 18; Pexels/RDNE Stock project, 12, 13, 19; Shutterstock/Andrea Raffin, 21, GoodStudio, 15, Kathy Hutchins, 21, Krakenimages.com, 7, nikiteev_konstantin, 22, 23, Vladimir Vasiltvich, 9; Wikimedia Commons/Cecilia Wang, 21

# CHAPTER ONE

# Why are martial arts called "arts" and not "sports"?

Martial arts are **visual arts**. The moves can look like a dance. The end goal is not violence. Instead, students focus on **self-discipline**. The physical skills are used for **self-defense**.

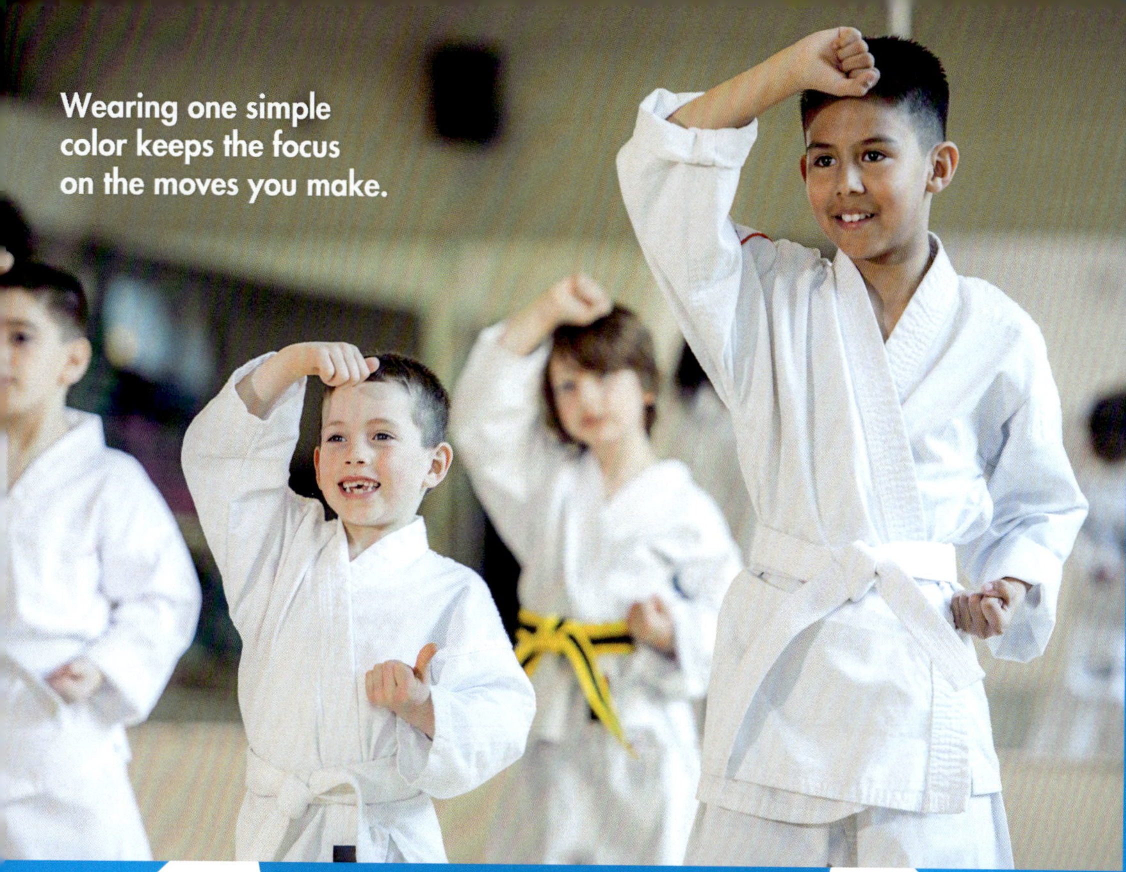

Wearing one simple color keeps the focus on the moves you make.

## DID YOU KNOW?

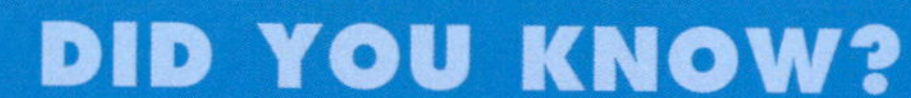

**Most martial arts today started in China, Korea, and Japan.**

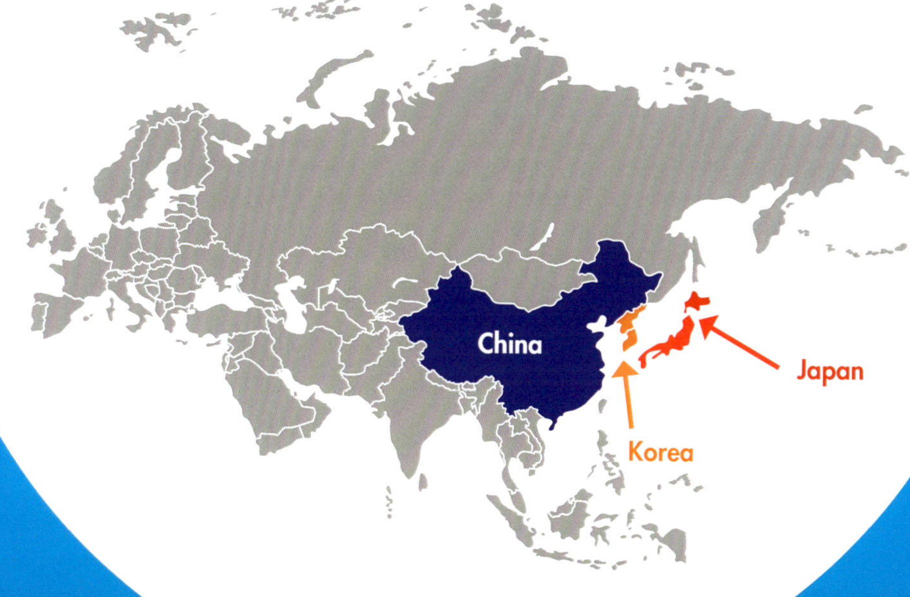

# What is a gi?

A **gi** is a uniform. It has loose pants and a shirt to let you move easily. A gi is usually white, blue, or black. You'll wear a colored belt with it. The belt shows your level of skill. Beginners wear white belts. The highest level is usually a black belt.

**DID YOU KNOW?**

**Taekwondo uses protective gear for sparring. There is a padded helmet and vest. Students also wear gloves and foot protection.**

Padded Helmet

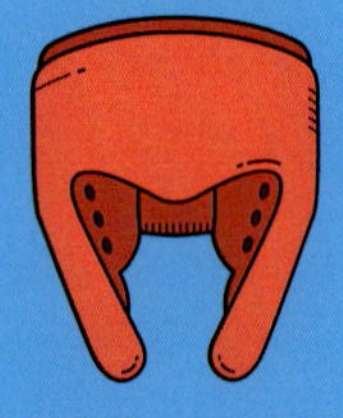

Padded Vest

Gloves

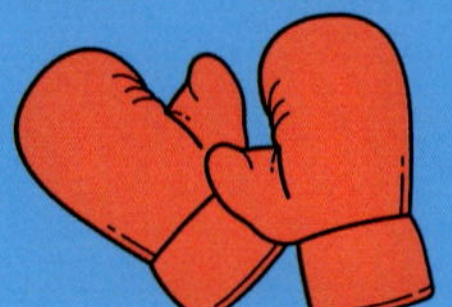

It takes a lot of training to earn a black belt.

Karate focuses on using your hands and legs as weapons.

# Will I use weapons?

Kyudo uses a bow and arrow.

Kendo uses wooden swords and sometimes armor.

Most styles don't use weapons. You use your body. "Karate" even means "empty hand." But some martial arts use tools. Kyudo uses bows and arrows. Kendo uses wooden swords. You'll need a mouthguard for sparring.

Sparring is part of Taekwondo competitions.

# What is a dojo?

Bowing to your opponent before a match is an act of respect.

A **dojo** is a large space. It may be a gym or a whole building. It's where you'll have class. You'll work on your skills there. It has mirrors to watch your moves. Padded floors help keep you from getting hurt.

You can start martial arts at any age.

# When can I start martial arts?

Right now! Some dojos have short classes for preschoolers. Many kids join at age six. It is a good way to gain strength and **confidence**. Make sure you can pay attention. The instructor will teach you simple moves to start.

# Which style is the best for me?

**Learning balance is important for different styles of martial arts.**

Pick one that is fun! It should challenge you, too. You can try different styles. Taekwondo makes your legs stronger. You will learn kicks and balance. You will also learn **mindfulness**. Judo teaches you how to pin someone to the ground. It also teaches hard work and **honor**. You could try more than one!

1
JIU JITSU
GRAPPLING OR PINNING
2
KARATE
STRIKING AND BLOCKING
3
TAEKWONDO
KICKS
4
JUDO
GRAPPLING OR PINNING
5
AIKIDO
THROWING, STRIKING, PINNING

CHAPTER THREE

Competing allows you to put your skills to the test.

# Do I have to compete?

Watching competitions can help you learn more about different styles of martial arts.

**DID YOU KNOW?**
**Taekwondo is the latest martial art to join the Olympics. It was added in 2000.**

No. But it's a big part of martial arts. You get to show how much you've learned. Competing helps you learn to deal with stress. You also get to watch and learn from others. Competitions help you become a better martial artist.

Instructors challenge you to improve your skills.

# Who will teach me?

Someone who knows the style well. Most instructors have multiple black belts. Find an instructor you feel comfortable with. They will teach you in class and coach you at competitions. Your instructor should be positive and inspire you!

Your instructor will teach you all of the physical and mental skills you need.

# Can I get a black belt?

There are different colors of belts. Each color is a different level.

Yes, if you work hard! You take belt tests to get to the next level. You will answer questions and show your skills. It takes years to get a black belt. It is hard work. You will need to pass a lot of tests. But it's worth it. Martial arts help your body and mind get stronger!

## FAMOUS MARTIAL ARTISTS

Bruce Lee

Donnie Yen

Jackie Chan

Chuck Norris

Jessie Graff

## ASK MORE QUESTIONS

**Do I wear shoes?**

**How is karate different from other martial arts?**

**Try a BIG QUESTION: How does a martial art keep your mind and body healthy?**

## SEARCH FOR ANSWERS

**Search the library catalog or the Internet.**
A librarian, teacher, or parent can help you.

**Using Keywords**
Find the looking glass.

**Keywords are the most important words in your question.**

**If you want to know about:**

- if you wear shoes, type: WEAR SHOES IN MARTIAL ARTS
- how karate is different, type: KARATE VS TAEKWONDO

# LEARN MORE

## FIND GOOD SOURCES

**Here are some good, safe sources you can use in your research.**
Your librarian can help you find more.

### Books

**Get Active!: Martial Arts**
by Alix Wood, 2022.

**Martial Arts Fun**
by Cari Meister, 2021.

### Internet Sites

**Martial Art**
*https://kids.britannica.com/kids/article/martial-art/353438*
This encyclopedia site focuses on the basics of martial arts.

**Taekwondo**
*https://www.paris2024.org/en/sport/taekwondo/*
This Olympics site has information about taekwondo at the 2024 Games. It includes rules, history, and events.

Every effort has been made to ensure that these websites are appropriate for children. However, because of the nature of the Internet, it is impossible to guarantee that these sites will remain active indefinitely or that their contents will not be altered.

## SHARE AND TAKE ACTION

**Go to a dojo to watch a class.**
Watch students with different belt rankings and ask them what they like about martial arts.

**Take a class with a friend.**
See what you like and don't like about different styles of martial arts.

**Attend a competition.**
Take note of new moves you want to learn to improve your skills.

# GLOSSARY

**confidence** A feeling or belief that you can do something well.

**dojo** A school for teaching people different forms of martial arts.

**gi** A lightweight two-piece uniform, usually loose-fitting pants and a jacket, worn with a cloth belt.

**honor** High moral standards of behavior.

**mindfulness** To be aware of one's thoughts, emotions, and experiences.

**self-defense** Skills that make you capable of protecting yourself during an attack.

**self-discipline** The ability to make yourself do things that should be done.

**spar** To fight with someone as a form of training or practice.

**visual art** Creative art whose products are to be appreciated by sight.

# INDEX



## About the Author

Lisa M. Bolt Simons is a writer and retired educator living in Minnesota. She never took a martial arts class but thinks she should after researching this book. She was a sports mom to her twins, Jeri and Anthony, for more than a decade and loves writing books for kids.